The Journey to World's End

Adapted by Tisha Hamilton

Based on characters created by Ted Elliott & Terry Rossio
and Stuart Beattie and Jay Wolpert
Written by Ted Elliott & Terry Rossio
Based on Walt Disney's Pirates of the Caribbean
Produced by Jerry Bruckheimer
Directed by Gore Verbinski

Part One

Reader's Digest
Children's Books

Pleasantville, New York • Montréal, Québec • Bath, United Kingdom

INTRODUCTION

DISK 1

Not too long ago, Captain Jack Sparrow found himself in search of a ship in the town of Port Royal. His own ship, the *Black Pearl*, had been taken from him by his mutinous first mate, Barbossa. But the joke was

on Barbossa. Why? Because the greedy pirate had stolen a chest full of cursed Aztec Gold that turned his crew into the living dead. They would be cursed to sail the seas without the joys of the living until all the gold was returned.

But Sparrow was not bothered by the curse and was determined to get his ship back. In Port Royal, he commandeered one of the Royal Navy's fastest vessels—the *Intercepter*—with

the reluctant help of one William Turner. Turner was a local swordsmith who only helped Sparrow for one

reason—Elizabeth Swann.

The young daughter of Governor Swann was Turner's true love. She had rescued him from the sea

DISK 2

when he was a young boy. Sadly, since then she had become betrothed to Commodore Norrington. Later, however, Barbossa and his men had arrived in Port Royal and taken her captive. The reason? She wore the last piece of the Aztec Gold around her neck.

So together, Jack and Will went after Barbossa—Jack went to get back his ship. Will went

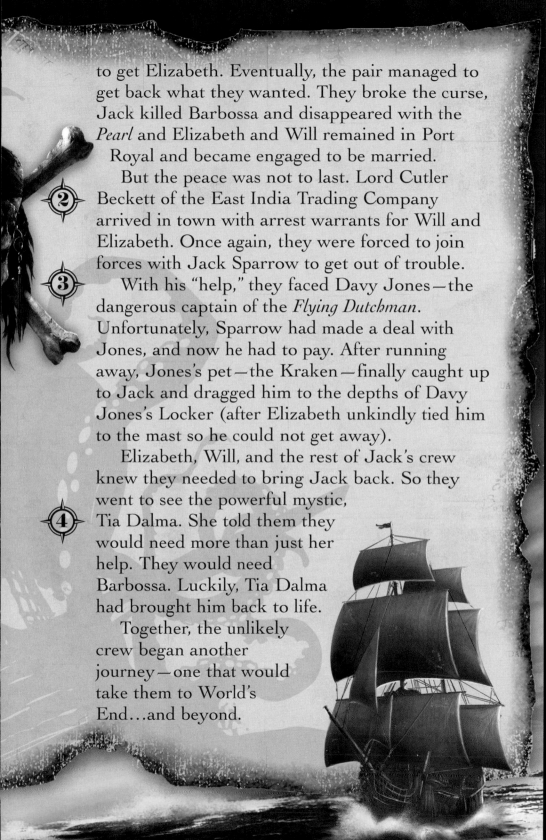

to get Elizabeth. Eventually, the pair managed to get back what they wanted. They broke the curse, Jack killed Barbossa and disappeared with the *Pearl* and Elizabeth and Will remained in Port Royal and became engaged to be married.

②　But the peace was not to last. Lord Cutler Beckett of the East India Trading Company arrived in town with arrest warrants for Will and Elizabeth. Once again, they were forced to join forces with Jack Sparrow to get out of trouble.

③　With his "help," they faced Davy Jones—the dangerous captain of the *Flying Dutchman*. Unfortunately, Sparrow had made a deal with Jones, and now he had to pay. After running away, Jones's pet—the Kraken—finally caught up to Jack and dragged him to the depths of Davy Jones's Locker (after Elizabeth unkindly tied him to the mast so he could not get away).

Elizabeth, Will, and the rest of Jack's crew knew they needed to bring Jack back. So they went to see the powerful mystic, ④ Tia Dalma. She told them they would need more than just her help. They would need Barbossa. Luckily, Tia Dalma had brought him back to life.

Together, the unlikely crew began another journey—one that would take them to World's End...and beyond.

It wasn't a great time to be a pirate. Jack Sparrow and his ship, the *Black Pearl*, had been dragged down to the depths of Davy Jones's Locker by the beastly Kraken. Elizabeth Swann and Will Turner had barely escaped with their lives. The East India Trading Company was capturing pirates all over the world and exacting its ruthless penalty: death.

Singapore was different. The docks and city were controlled by the Pirate Lord, Captain Sao Feng. It was risky, but Elizabeth and Barbossa needed to see him.

"I find myself in need of a ship and crew," Barbossa told Sao Feng.

"What a coincidence," Sao Feng observed dryly. Then he signaled one of his bodyguards to bring out a prisoner. It was Will Turner! "We caught him stealing

navigational charts to the Farthest Gate," Sao Feng explained. "Is that where you're planning to take this ship and crew?"

The Farthest Gate led to Davy Jones's Locker... and Jack Sparrow.

Barbossa explained. The Brethren Court had been called. The Court was made up of nine Pirate Lords who established—and enforced—the rules that all pirates lived by. "Lord Cutler Beckett and the East India Trading Company challenge our rule of the sea," Barbossa told him. "We need to fight back."

"And Jack Sparrow is one of the nine," Will said. "We need to bring him back."

At the mention of Jack Sparrow's name, Sao Feng's expression darkened. Before he could say anything, he spied a traitor in their midst. Suddenly, everyone had their weapons drawn. Moments later, agents of the East India Trading Company burst in.

DISK 4

Thanks to some extra help from Tia Dalma and Jack's remaining crew, the pirates managed to win the fight. Will struck a secret deal with Sao Feng. When Barbossa and Elizabeth caught up with him on the docks, he had the charts and a ship, the *Hai Peng*, and a crew, too. Sao Feng and his men would cover their escape, and then he would meet up with them. But what had Will promised in exchange? And why?

As the exotic-looking Chinese junk sailed out of the harbor, fires from the recent battle smoldered into the night sky. Elizabeth and Tia Dalma shared a quiet moment on deck.

"There be something on the seas that even the staunchest pirates have come to fear," Tia Dalma warned as they drifted toward their next adventure.

What was it the pirates feared? The *Flying Dutchman*. Lord Beckett arranged a meeting with Davy Jones on his otherworldly ship, the *Dutchman*.

DISK 5

Norrington and his men carried a chest on board, and even the terrifying Davy Jones kept his distance from it. The chest held the still-beating heart of Davy Jones, and Beckett was using it to control him.

Meanwhile, as the *Hai Peng* continued on its journey, the seas surrounding it grew ever more ghostly. Clouds and snow swirled around the ship and soon huge icebergs appeared. Still the *Hai Peng* sailed on. After the ice, the sea grew dark. Will gradually became aware of a roaring sound. The ship began to turn on its own as if pulled toward the sound. Elizabeth looked at Will with alarm. What were they in for now?

The ship began to pick up speed as it headed toward an endless waterfall, where the edge of the ocean flowed down into a billowing mist of nothingness. They were at World's End. Only Tia Dalma seemed calm and at peace as she surveyed their impending doom. Casually, she tossed some crab claws onto a barrel and began to murmur something in a foreign language.

The hull of the *Hai Peng* now jutted over the horrifying abyss. Then it began to tilt over the edge. In the moment before it fell, Elizabeth's scream pierced the air and was answered by Barbossa's throaty laugh.

Jack Sparrow stood on the deck of the *Black Pearl*. But in the white-hot afterworld of Davy Jones's Locker, the ship teetered not on the water, but on an infinite sea of sand. Jack was marooned on his unmoving ship in a blank and windless eternity: a pirate's nightmare. Suddenly, the *Black Pearl* began to move as a wave of thousands of chittering crabs carried it across the blazing sand.

Not too far away, the crew of the destroyed *Hai Peng* staggered from the wreckage onto the shore of Davy Jones's Locker. Tia Dalma held out her arm. A crab scuttled up, followed by another. Then came the *Black Pearl* sailing across the sand and splashing into the waves, Jack at its helm.

Elizabeth was glad to see Jack. After all, *she* was the one who had tied him to the *Pearl's* mast right before the Kraken pulled it under. Jack, on the other hand, wasn't so sure how he felt about everything. True, he'd been rescued from a terrifying oblivion, but now he had to deal with Barbossa again. He and Barbossa quickly began to bicker about who would captain the *Black Pearl*.

Will stepped in, explaining that Beckett held the heart of Davy Jones and was now taking control over the very ocean itself.

"The Brethren Court has been called," Tia Dalma told him. Jack agreed to go back — and let everyone come. Soon the *Black Pearl's* eerie journey back to the land of the living was underway.

It seemed as if the *Black Pearl* would be stuck between worlds forever, but Jack finally figured out a way out of their predicament. He started running from side to side. Everyone started doing the same until finally the *Black Pearl* spun right under the water. When it whirled up into the air again, they were in the land of the living.

The first order of business was finding a fresh water supply. Will used Sao Feng's charts to find a tiny island. When they arrived, they found the Kraken dead on its shore. Yet there was worse to come. Sao Feng had caught up to them. His pirates took over the *Pearl*!

It turned out this was part of the deal Will had made with Sao Feng. Now Will would captain the *Pearl*, while his crew was taken away in chains.

Then the *Endeavour* sailed up and Beckett came aboard to take Jack prisoner. It seemed as if things could get no worse.

Meanwhile, more wheeling and dealing began on board the *Pearl* between Sao Feng and Barbossa. Sao Feng agreed to let Jack's crew go—on one condition. Elizabeth would have to stay with him on his ship, the *Empress*. "Done," Elizabeth agreed without hesitating. Will was dismayed, but Elizabeth had to do it.

DISK 7

When they got aboard the *Empress*, Sao Feng treated Elizabeth like a goddess. Little did she know he actually believed she was a goddess. Barbossa had convinced him that Elizabeth was really Calypso, a legendary goddess of the seas. Long ago, Calypso had been captured by the nine original Pirate Lords. Then they had imprisoned her in an earthly form.

As the *Empress* sailed away, Jack and Beckett emerged onto the deck of the *Endeavour*. That's when Jack saw the *Pearl*.

Beckett's men had tried to take it over, but thanks to Sao Feng, the crew of the *Pearl* was taking it back. As his ship drifted further and further away, Jack quickly rigged a contraption to get him across the water and onto the *Pearl*. Unfortunately for Beckett, it involved firing a cannonball through the mast of the *Endeavour*. Jack used the recoil of the cannon blast to propel himself out over the sea and onto the deck of the *Pearl*.

Once aboard the *Pearl*, Jack wasted no time. "Take this traitor to the brig," he barked as Will was led away. They were on their way to Shipwreck Cove. And thanks to Jack's clever cannonball trick, the *Endeavour* wouldn't be able to follow for a while.

勒比海盗王

Aboard the *Empress*, Elizabeth and Sao Feng were getting to know one another. Elizabeth now realized that Sao Feng thought she was Calypso. She played along, and in the process learned much about the lore of the Pirate Lords—until a cannonball rudely interrupted the proceedings. The *Flying Dutchman* was attacking the *Empress*. In the explosion, Sao Feng was hurt.

Sao Feng fumbled with the intricate rope knot he always wore around his neck. "The Captain's Knot," he said. Then he took it off and gave it to Elizabeth. She was now captain of the *Empress*. It was time to face her ship's attackers.

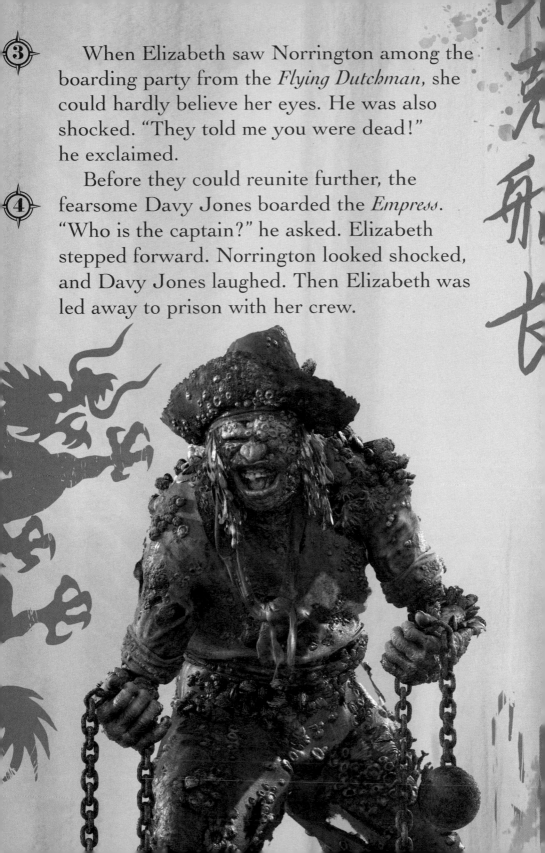

3 When Elizabeth saw Norrington among the boarding party from the *Flying Dutchman*, she could hardly believe her eyes. He was also shocked. "They told me you were dead!" he exclaimed.

4 Before they could reunite further, the fearsome Davy Jones boarded the *Empress*. "Who is the captain?" he asked. Elizabeth stepped forward. Norrington looked shocked, and Davy Jones laughed. Then Elizabeth was led away to prison with her crew.

Behind bars in the brig on the *Flying Dutchman*, Elizabeth suddenly remembered Will's father was part of the crew. "Bootstrap?" she murmured. A pair of eyes opened in the ship's hull. It was "Bootstrap Bill" Turner himself. But he no longer looked human. He now seemed to be a part of the ship.

"You know my name," he said.

"I know your son," she told him. Bootstrap was overjoyed to hear that Will had indeed made a safe escape from his last encounter with the *Flying Dutchman* and was alive and well. "He's coming to save you," she added.

"He can't," Bootstrap said simply. "If Jones be slain, he who slays him takes his place as captain of the *Dutchman* forever after. If he saves me, he loses you. Tell him not to come. It's too late. I'm part of the ship now." With that, Bootstrap closed his strange eyes.

Back aboard the *Endeavour*, Beckett was making a discovery of his own as he tried to find the *Black Pearl*! Looking over the railing, he saw two barrels floating by. There was also a note bearing the symbol of the East India Trading Company.

"We are meant to follow," Beckett said. Then he smiled cruelly. "Adjust course, Lieutenant."

Jack came upon Will as he was preparing another pair of barrels. Will was betraying the *Pearl*. He thought that if he led Beckett to Shipwreck Cove, Beckett would free Bootstrap, his father. Jack persuaded him to try another plan. Jack himself would slay the beating heart of Davy Jones and take his place at the helm of the *Flying Dutchman*. That way, Jack would never die. He had already been dead and he knew he didn't like it one bit.

DISK 8

①

He handed Will his Compass, saying, "Here. Be sure to give Davy Jones my regards." Then he pushed Will overboard! Ever thoughtful, though, Jack also threw some barrels overboard as well. This way, Will could at least stay afloat and keep breathing air instead of water.

In the *Dutchman's* brig, Elizabeth's eyes sprang open when she heard a clinking sound. To her surprise, it was Norrington unlocking her cell. "Be quiet," he said. "This way. Hurry." She saw that he'd also freed the other crewmen from the *Empress*, which bobbed along behind the *Flying Dutchman* on a towline. She didn't notice that Bootstrap had followed them.

One at a time, the crew crawled along the towline to reach their ship. Norrington warned Elizabeth against heading for Shipwreck Cove.

"Beckett knows everything. I fear you have a traitor in your midst," he explained. Elizabeth implored him to join her on the *Empress*.

Just then, Bootstrap spoke up. "Who goes there?" he asked. Norrington tried to hold him off while Elizabeth crawled across the rope to safety on the *Empress*. But as Bootstrap began to raise an alarm, she was only halfway across. Norrington boldly shot his pistol to break the towline. Still clutching the rope, Elizabeth splashed into the water, but she—and the *Empress*— were free!

...continued in Part Two